DRAGONFLY BOOKS

This Dragonfly Book belongs to:

_____

allow children to think . . . to imagine . . . to dream.

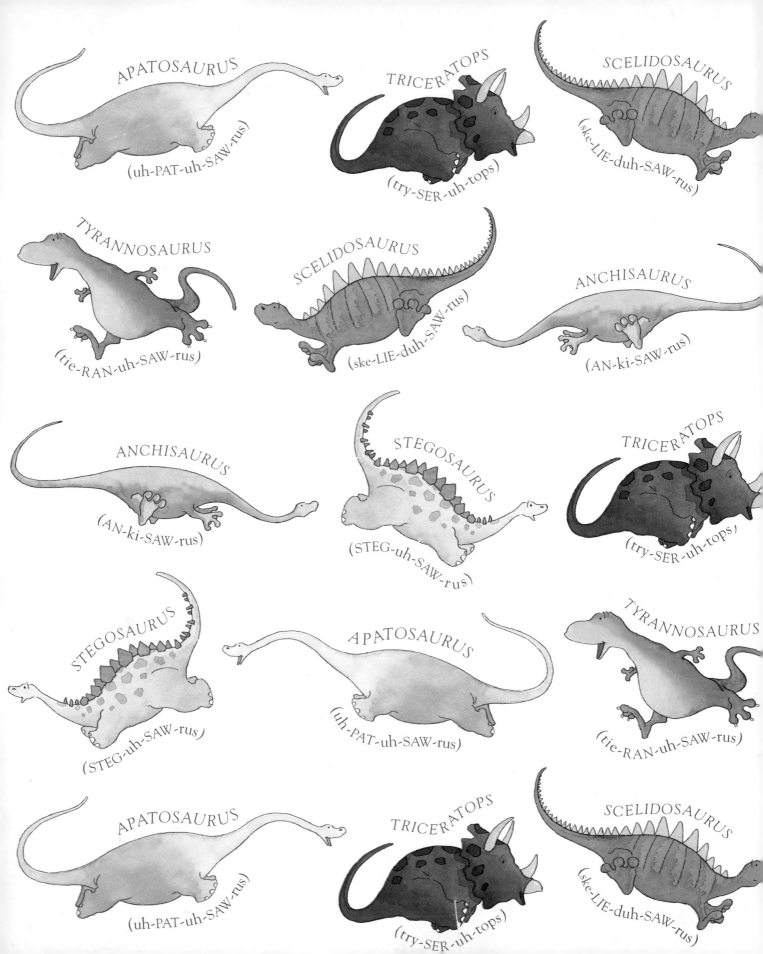

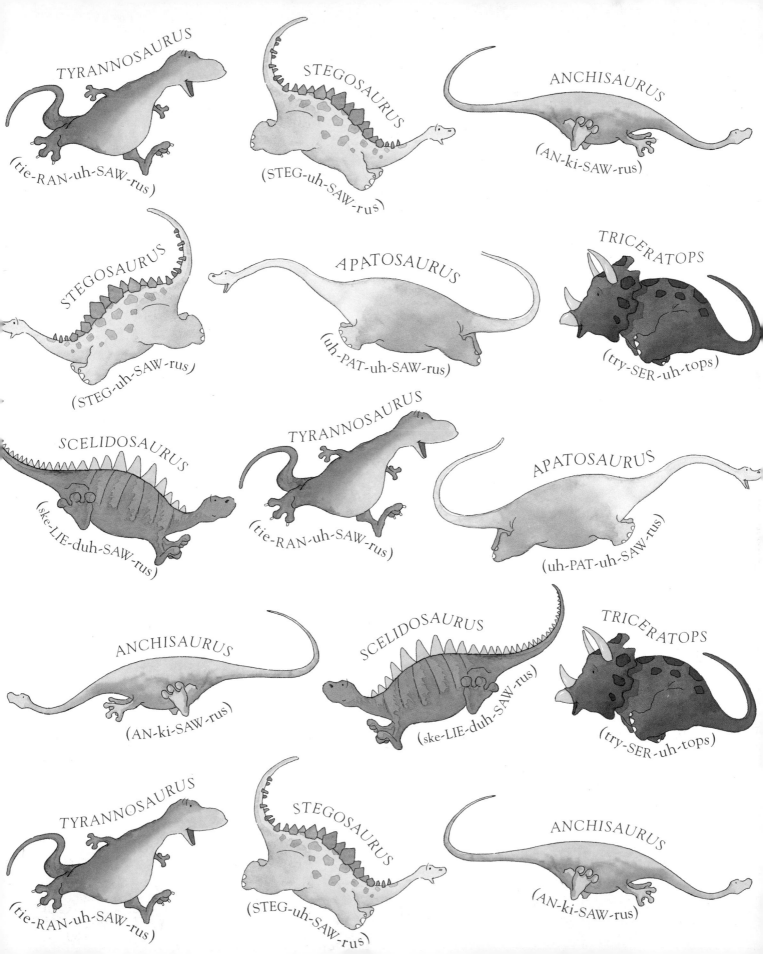

For Thomas Owlett,
who introduced his bucketful of dinosaurs
to Ann and me one lucky Sunday afternoon
at The Chelsea Gardener
—I.W.

For William
—A.R.

With thanks to Dr. Angela Milner
at the Natural History Museum, London

Text copyright © 1999 by Ian Whybrow
Illustrations copyright © 1999 by Adrian Reynolds

Visit us on the Web! www.randomhouse.com/kids

Educators and librarians, for a variety of teaching tools,
visit us at www.randomhouse.com/teachers

The Library of Congress has cataloged the hardcover edition of this work as follows:

Whybrow, Ian.
Harry and the bucketful of dinosaurs / by Ian Whybrow ; illustrated by Adrian Reynolds.
p. cm.
Summary: Harry finds toy dinosaurs in the attic that come to life when he names each one.
ISBN 978-0-375-82541-5 (trade)
[1. Dinosaurs—Fiction. 2. Toys—Fiction.] I. Reynolds, Adrian, ill. II. Title.

ISBN 978-0-375-85119-3 (pbk.)

MANUFACTURED IN CHINA

10 9 8 7 6 5 4 3 2

First Dragonfly Books Edition

Harry
and the
Bucketful *of*
Dinosaurs

Written by Ian Whybrow
Illustrated by Adrian Reynolds

Dragonfly Books ⸺ New York

Gran thought the attic needed cleaning out.
She let Harry help.
Harry found an old box
all covered with dust.

He lifted the lid . . .
DINOSAURS!

Harry took the
dinosaurs downstairs.

He unbent the
bent ones.

He fixed the
broken ones.

He got up on a chair and washed them in the sink.
Gran came to see. "Just what do
you think you're up to?" she asked.

"Dinosaurs don't like boxes," Harry said.
"They want to be in a bucket."

Sam came in from watching TV.
She said it was stupid, fussing over so much junk.
"Dinosaurs aren't junk," Harry said.

The next day, Harry went to the library with Mom.
He took the dinosaurs in their bucket.

He found out all the names in a book
and told them to the dinosaurs.
He whispered to each one:
"You are my Scelidosaurus."
"You are my Stegosaurus."
"You are my Triceratops."

And there were enough names for all of the dinosaurs:
the Apatosaurus, the Anchisaurus, and the Tyrannosaurus.
The dinosaurs said, "Thank you, Harry."
They said it very quietly,
but just loud enough for Harry to hear.

After that, the dinosaurs went everywhere with Harry.

They went shopping.

They went to the
garden center.

Sometimes they got left behind.
But they were never lost for long
because Harry knew all their names.

And he always called out their names
just to make sure they were safe.

One day, Harry went on a train with Gran.
He was so excited, he forgot all about the bucket.

Gran dried his eyes.
"Never mind," she said.
"I'll buy you a nice, new video."

Harry watched the video with Sam.
It was nice, but not like the dinosaurs.

At bedtime, Harry said to Mom,
"I like videos. But I like my dinosaurs better
because you can fix them, you can bathe them,
you can take them to bed.

And best of all, you can say their names."

Harry was still upset at breakfast the next morning.
Sam said, "Dusty old junk!"
That was why Sam's book got milk on it.
Gran took Harry to his room to settle down.

Later, Gran took Harry back to the train station
to see the Lost and Found Man.
The man said, "Dinosaurs? Yes, we have found some dinosaurs.
But how do we know they are *your* dinosaurs?"

Harry said, "I will close
my eyes and call their names.
Then you will know."

And Harry closed his eyes and called their names.
He called:

"Come back

my Scelidosaurus!"

"Come back, my Stegosaurus!"

"Come back, my Triceratops!"

He called, "Come back" to all the dinosaurs:
   the Apatosaurus
      and the Anchisaurus
      and the Tyrannosaurus
      and all of the lost old dinosaurs.
And when he opened his eyes . . .

. . . there they were—all of them,
standing on the counter next to the bucket!
"All correct!" said the man.
"These are definitely your dinosaurs. *Definitely!*"

And the dinosaurs whispered to Harry.
They whispered very quietly,
but just loud enough for Harry to hear.
"You are definitely our Harry, *definitely!*"

Going home from the station,
Harry was very happy.
Gran said to the neighbor,
"Our Harry likes those old dinosaurs."

"Definitely," whispered Harry.
"And my dinosaurs *definitely* like me!"
ENDOSAURUS

APATOSAURUS
(uh-PAT-uh-SAW-rus)

TRICERATOPS
(try-SER-uh-tops)

SCELIDOSAURUS
(ske-LIE-duh-SAW-rus)

TYRANNOSAURUS
(tie-RAN-uh-SAW-rus)

SCELIDOSAURUS
(ske-LIE-duh-SAW-rus)

ANCHISAURUS
(AN-ki-SAW-rus)

ANCHISAURUS
(AN-ki-SAW-rus)

STEGOSAURUS
(STEG-uh-SAW-rus)

TRICERATOPS
(try-SER-uh-tops)

STEGOSAURUS
(STEG-uh-SAW-rus)

APATOSAURUS
(uh-PAT-uh-SAW-rus)

TYRANNOSAURUS
(tie-RAN-uh-SAW-rus)

APATOSAURUS
(uh-PAT-uh-SAW-rus)

TRICERATOPS
(try-SER-uh-tops)

SCELIDOSAURUS
(ske-LIE-duh-SAW-rus)

TYRANNOSAURUS
(tie-RAN-uh-SAW-rus)

STEGOSAURUS
(STEG-uh-SAW-rus)

ANCHISAURUS
(AN-ki-SAW-rus)

STEGOSAURUS
(STEG-uh-SAW-rus)

APATOSAURUS
(uh-PAT-uh-SAW-rus)

TRICERATOPS
(try-SER-uh-tops)

SCELIDOSAURUS
(ske-LIE-duh-SAW-rus)

TYRANNOSAURUS
(tie-RAN-uh-SAW-rus)

APATOSAURUS
(uh-PAT-uh-SAW-rus)

ANCHISAURUS
(AN-ki-SAW-rus)

SCELIDOSAURUS
(ske-LIE-duh-SAW-rus)

TRICERATOPS
(try-SER-uh-tops)

TYRANNOSAURUS
(tie-RAN-uh-SAW-rus)

STEGOSAURUS
(STEG-uh-SAW-rus)

ANCHISAURUS
(AN-ki-SAW-rus)

DRAGONFLY
BOOKS

Dragonfly Books introduce children
to the pleasures of caring about and sharing books.
With Dragonfly Books, children will discover
talented artists and writers and
the worlds they have created,
ranging from first concept books to
read-together stories to books for
newly independent readers.

One of the best gifts a child can receive
is a book to read and enjoy.
Sharing reading with children today
benefits them now and in the future.

Begin building your child's future . . .
one Dragonfly Book at a time.

For help in selecting books, look for these themes
on the back cover of every Dragonfly Book:

CLASSICS (Including Caldecott Award Winners)
CONCEPTS (Alphabet, Counting, and More)
CULTURAL DIVERSITY
DEATH AND DYING
FAMILY
FASCINATING PEOPLE
FRIENDSHIP
GROWING UP
JUST FOR FUN
MYTHS AND LEGENDS
NATURE AND OUR ENVIRONMENT
OUR HISTORY (Nonfiction and Historical Fiction)
POETRY
SCHOOL
SPORTS